SERIES CAN

JUMP START

by Sylvia McNicoll

Should I tell him why I never looked at books? Did I have the guts?

"I don't care if I ever finish school," I said instead.

"Of course you're going to finish," Dad thundered. "What kind of job do you think you can get as a high school dropout?"

"Mechanic," I said quietly. Then I took a deep breath and told him again, "I'm going to be a mechanic."

How many **Series Canada** titles have you read?

AMY'S WISH
BABY, BABY
BREAK OUT
BURN OUT
DEAD ON
DIRT BIKE
DOPE DEAL
FAIR PLAY
FIRE! FIRE!
GANG WAR
GET LOST
HEAD LOCK
HOT CARS
ICE HAWK
METAL HEAD
MICRO MAN
NINE LIVES
NO WAY
REBEL YELL
RUNAWAY
SNOW GHOST
SPIN OUT
SPLIT UP
TAKE OFF
THE BEAST
THE WIMP
TOUGH STUFF
WILD NIGHT
WILD ONE

SERIES CANADA

For my readers at
St. Elizabeth

SYLVIA McNICOLL

JUMP START

Because everyone needs
a jump start sometimes

Sylvia McNicoll

November 4, 1992

Collier Macmillan Canada, Inc.

Collier Macmillan Canada, Inc.
1200 Eglinton Ave. East, Suite 200
Don Mills, Ontario M3C 3N1

ISBN0-02-953928-5

General Editor: Paul Kropp
Series Editor: Sandra Gulland
Title Editor: Glenn Woods
Designer: Brant Cowie
Illustrator: Janet Wilson
Cover Photograph: Paterson Photographic

1 2 3 4 5 6 93 92 91 90 89
Printed and bound in Canada

CANADIAN CATALOGUING IN PUBLICATION DATA

McNicoll, Sylvia, 1954-
    Jump start

(Series Canada)
ISBN 0-02-953928-5

I. Title.   II. Series.

PS.8575.N53J85 1989 jC813'.54 C89-095045-8
PZ7.M265Ju 1989

CONTENTS

CHAPTER

"Same old stuff," Dad said. He flicked the back of his hand against my report card. "Here you are in high school with a fresh start and what do you do? Look at these marks. Are you proud of this?"

I didn't think I was supposed to answer that, and I was right.

"You're failing English, and you'll have to stay behind another year. Is that what you really want?"

He didn't wait for an answer this time either. "I know you can do better than this, Shari. You don't apply yourself. I never see you even looking at a book.

You'll never finish high school at this rate."

Should I tell him why I never looked at books? Did I have the guts?

"I don't care if I ever finish school," I said instead.

"Of course you're going to finish," Dad thundered. "What kind of job do you think you can get as a high school dropout?"

"Mechanic," I said quietly. Then I took a deep breath and told him again, "I'm going to be a mechanic."

Dad's face went purple. "A mechanic? My daughter—pumping gas at some dirty garage?"

"But Dad, I—"

"But nothing. That boyfriend of yours is giving you these ideas," Dad shouted, his fist smashing down on the coffee table. "Well, it's going to stop!"

"No!" I shouted back. I *had* to make him listen.

"What?" Dad said in his how-dare-you voice.

"It has nothing to do with Hank," I said softly. "It's just, well—you know I like to fix things."

"Well, fix your marks then," he yelled, "because until you do, you're grounded." He flung my report card at me.

"Now go to your room," he said, "and read a book for a change."

I can't read, I wanted to shout. That's what I really needed to tell him. But instead I walked off to my room and sat down to a desk full of books. Lyn, my only friend in Kamloops, kept giving me her old Sun Valley High paperbacks. And I kept taking the books home. I didn't want Lyn or the other kids to know I couldn't read.

I opened *Jane Eyre*, the book we were studying in English.

"Read the first five chapters for next class," Mr. Fulmer had told us. The rest of the kids shut their books, yawned, and rolled their eyes. I pretended to be bored too. All I really wanted was to fit in.

But now here I was with the book open, hoping my usual hope—that reading would suddenly work for me.

No such luck.

THERE SAW ON POSSIBILITY TAKING A WALK DAY, I made out. The tiny print looked like ants crawling

across the page. SAW, SAW? No—that word must be WAS. I ran my finger under the next word to make it stop moving and blurring. Was that word really ON or was it NO? The line didn't make sense either way.

My eyes burned and I shut the book. *Why am I so stupid?* I wondered for the millionth time.

I flung down *Jane Eyre* and pushed all the other books off my desk. One old picture book landed near my feet— *Sleeping Beauty*. I used to make Dad read it over and over. Then one time I "read" it back to him.

"She can read, she can read!" Dad cried out as he dashed to Mom's office in the den. "Just come and listen to her." He dragged Mom away from her work.

"And she's only four!" he said when I had finished the story.

Mom smiled and turned the book right side up before she went back to her work. That was a different time, a different house. They weren't so busy then and I wasn't in school yet. Back then, my father thought I was great—but not any more. *You're not paying attention in class,* Dad would tell me now. *You aren't working hard enough.*

I picked up *Sleeping Beauty* and stared at the cover. The prince was kneeling beside the princess to kiss her awake. *If only that would happen to me,* I thought—*and soon.*

CHAPTER 2

I heard knocking, so I scrambled to pick up the books. When I opened the door, I found Mom standing there with hot chocolate and cookies on a tray.

"Mom, I'm just not very smart," I said, taking the tray from her.

"Don't say that, Shari. You're clever about so many things."

"Yeah, but not in school."

"Well, just don't give up," Mom said, "and keep on trying your best."

"Sure," I said. I sipped at the hot chocolate and ate a cookie. Mom smiled, touched my shoulder, and left the room.

Same old story—try your best. Didn't Mom know that my best just wasn't good enough?

I felt so rotten I started to cry. Only one person could make me feel better—my boyfriend Hank. Grounded or not, I had to see him.

I took out my biggest teddy bear from the closet. Fluffy still came in handy at times like this. I stuffed him under the covers and flicked off the light.

"Good night, Mom," I called out, one leg already over the window ledge.

"Good night, Shari."

My other leg went over the ledge and I jumped down.

Quickly I walked toward Vandyke's Garage. I knew Hank would still be working on his old Ford LTD—The Heap we called it. His dad would have gone home by now.

But halfway there, I heard a noise— the kind when someone tries and tries to start a car. The engine turns over, but it just won't catch. BRRRRANG, BRRRRANG, BRRRRANG. It sounded like a cat in pain.

"Drew, what are you doing? You're

killing your starter," I called out when I saw the car. It was an orange Trans Am that belonged to the only eighteen-year-old in grade nine English.

"C'mon Shari, you still playing Fix-it Lady?" Drew snapped.

"Just pop the hood and let me have a look."

Drew rolled his eyes at me, but he pulled the hood release and I unlatched it.

He got out of the car lazy and slow, like he did from his seat at school. Then he walked around to where I stood. By that time I had taken off the air cleaner and

was checking the choke.

"Try it again," I said.

Drew shrugged his shoulders, walked back, and got in the car. I pushed a ballpoint pen against the choke plate to open it up, and the Trans Am started right up.

I walked around to his window and told him, "Your choke's just sticky."

"Hey thanks, Babe," he said, flooring it.

I jerked away and the Trans Am shot off.

Greaseball! Turkey! How could he drive a car like that and not know a thing about it? How could he even afford the gas for it?

I walked the rest of the way to the garage. The bell on the door jingled as I pushed it open, but Hank didn't notice. He was bent over the front of The Heap.

"Whatcha doing?" I asked.

He straightened up, looked around at me and said, "Checking the dwell on the points."

I stood up on tiptoes and hugged him tightly then. I was too upset to tell him I'd been grounded.

"You'll get yourself dirty, Shari," he said.

"I don't mind getting dirty," I told him. Another guy would have answered back with a smart remark. I could just imagine what Drew would have said. But not Hank, and that's what I liked about him.

"She should run a lot smoother when I'm done," he said, bending over the car.

"Hank, this condenser looks old. Are you changing the points and not the condenser?"

Hank hit his head with his hand. He got a new condenser off the shelf and with a little work had it in place.

"Hank, do you think your dad would hire a girl as a mechanic?" I asked.

"Well, he doesn't need another mechanic—and besides, no girls ever apply."

"I'd like to apply."

"Why? When we get married, you can stay at home."

Stay at home! "But I want to be a mechanic. I . . . ." I was so angry I couldn't go on.

Then it hit me. He'd said, *When we get*

married! I really like Hank—I think I even love him—but marriage, whoa!

Hank pushed back his white blond hair, leaving a greasy streak on his forehead. Then he went back to setting the points. "Could you read the specs out to me from the manual over there?" Hank asked, pointing with his elbow.

An alarm went off in my head. *Read?* I couldn't, but I didn't want Hank to know.

"No, I won't. I don't want to be *just* a wife—I want to be a mechanic!" I shouted and slammed the manual shut.

Before Hank could straighten up and stop me, I turned and ran out the door.

CHAPTER

3

"Shari, I don't want to read this boring stuff," my sister said.

"Fine. Then I won't let you do any rug hooking."

Melody was ten and she was reading *Jane Eyre* out loud for me.

"Aw, c'mon, you promised . . . ."

"Oh no I didn't. I said only if you read the first three chapters."

"O.K., O.K.," Melody said and kept reading. Some of the words were long and she stumbled on them, but it was better than I could do.

"All right, that's enough," I said when

neither of us could take it any longer. "Let's check on supper."

"But what about the rug hooking?"

"Later," I said. "Now it's time to put the vegetables in the old west."

It was an old joke just between us but it made her smile. Once Mom had left me a note about what to make for supper. I had read it the crazy-mixed-up way I always did.

"Heat up the old west," I had read out loud.

"Heat up the old west?" Melody had checked out the note on the fridge. "Oh, Shari, it says to heat up the old *stew*. Mom means for us to eat last night's leftovers."

We both laughed a lot about that one and plenty of other notes like it. I always laughed hard and loud to cover how bad I felt.

We ran up the stairs to the kitchen. Melody helped chop up the carrots and potatoes so we'd be done faster. "O.K., put 'em in," I said, and she dumped them from the cutting board into the pot.

"Can we . . . ." Melody asked.

"Yeah, yeah, we can do the rug

hooking now—even though you owe me a chapter." Melody wasn't that bad a kid, but I always had to con her so she'd help me with my schoolwork. She ran off and brought me back the kit. I showed her how to loop the yarn over the hook and push it between the threads of the canvas.

The doorbell rang. "You're doing fine," I said. Then, when I saw Hank's LTD through the living room window, I ran to the door.

"Hank!"

"Hi, Shari," Hank said, blushing. "I'm sorry about last night. I never meant you *had* to stay home when we got married. I just meant you didn't have to worry about getting a job."

"I'm sorry I walked out," I said.

"And I know you'd make a great mechanic—really."

I kissed him then, but the kiss lasted one moment too long. Dad's black New Yorker rolled up next to The Heap. Dad stared at the two of us, then got out of the car and walked up the driveway.

Great. Dad already thought Hank was a sex maniac. Hank was eighteen, and

what else would he want with a fifteen-year-old girl?

"Hello, Hank," Dad said, smiling with clenched teeth.

Hank nodded and mumbled something. He started to reach out his hand to shake Dad's until he noticed some grease on his own fingers.

"Homework all done, Shari?" Dad asked me.

"Almost," I said. That was my usual answer.

"Well, did you forget our talk?" Dad asked.

"Yeah, I remember, but I'll just be a minute." I looked straight back into his angry eyes. I knew Dad wouldn't have a fight on the front step, so I was safe.

"Nice to see you again, sir," Hank said.

"Good-bye," Dad replied, not quite slamming the door behind him.

"Let's go for a walk . . . just to the corner," I said to Hank.

I held his hand as we walked down the street, not even looking up until we reached the corner. Then I had to say what I felt—out loud.

"I hate my father."

"C'mon Shari—"

You don't really mean that, would be his next words.

I kissed him, but he broke away.

"C'mon Shari, don't play this game." This time he had to clear his throat.

For me, it was no game—I needed to be loved. I looked at him and I knew my eyes were wet.

"Wait another year," he said, taking me in his arms, "and then I'll ask your father if we can get married."

Get married—this was the second time he'd said that. The idea wasn't sounding so strange any more.

"You coming to church with me this Sunday?" he asked.

"Church? No, I can't—I'm grounded." For a moment I was almost glad. The last time I'd gone with him I'd felt out of place with his family and the service and everything. "I had a blow-up with Dad over my report card and now I'm grounded till my grades go up."

"Till your grades go up?" Hank groaned.

"Yeah, I know that means forever."

"Look, try not to worry about it." Hank frowned. "We'll find a way to see each other anyway," he said.

We walked back to the house then and Hank quicky kissed me good-bye.

Now what would Dad have to say to me?

CHAPTER

Dad was in the kitchen with Melody, eating supper.

"Your dinner's on the counter, cold," Dad said when I came in. "Zap it for a minute in the microwave." Then he stopped buttering his Pillsbury roll. "Grounded means no dates, just in case we aren't clear on that point."

"Hank just came by," I said. "He didn't know I was grounded."

"You could have told him on the front steps, since you do so many other things out there."

The microwave bleeped then, so I took

out my supper and sat down next to Melody. Mom walked in looking tired.

"No time to change, just wash up and join us," Dad said to her.

Mom acted as though she didn't hear him. She kissed us all hello, then microwaved a plate of stew and sat down. "Hmm, good stew, Shari."

"I helped make it too," Melody told her.

"Have a roll," Dad said, coming out of his bad mood a bit. "I made them."

"The library called, Shari," Melody said between mouthfuls. "They have your tape."

"I should have known it wouldn't be a book," Dad said to Mom. "She goes to a library for music, do you believe it?"

"Isn't it wild what they have these days?" Mom said. "But Superior Video didn't have that movie you wanted, Shari."

Dad coughed and grabbed for his water.

"Thanks for trying, Mom." I had hoped there was an old movie of *Jane Eyre* and had asked her to check.

"I'll drive you to the library after supper, if you want," she said before she

bit into a roll.

"Great!" I needed to listen to *Jane Eyre* as soon as I could. Maybe if I had time, I'd listen to it twice.

"She hasn't finished her homework," Dad said in his dangerous tone.

"We won't be long," Mom answered, ignoring the message in his voice.

Dad gulped down his water.

"May I be excused then?" I said, mostly to Dad.

"Go," he answered.

I got my purse and a jacket from my room. Then I grabbed my Walkman and hung the earphones around my neck.

"Ready?" Mom asked when I passed the kitchen door.

Dad saw the Walkman. "Can't you wait till you're home to listen to it?"

"You don't have to use your Walkman," Mom said, "you can use the tape deck in the car."

"Uh, no, that's O.K." I said. Why did I feel like everyone was backing me into a corner?

"The music has to be blasting directly into her brain for her to enjoy it," Dad said.

Life would be easier if I could tell him—*This is my homework, Dad.* Instead I got him angrier and angrier at me. I looked down at the floor until Mom was ready. "C'mon let's go," she said, and we got into her yellow Subaru.

"Shari, were you really necking with Hank on the front step when your father came home?"

"One kiss and Dad calls it necking." I rolled my eyes and looked out the window.

Mom glanced over at me for a second and changed the subject. "What do you want for your sixteenth birthday?"

"Mom, what I'd really like—most in the world—is if you and Dad would let me take auto mechanics next term."

"Oh boy, that's a tough one," she said. "But who knows? We still have a couple of weeks to work on him." She winked at me.

When we got to the library, she checked on the movie while I picked up my tape. I put it in the Walkman right away.

It was a good way not to have to talk about school on the way home. The moment we got in the house though, I whipped my earphones off. I didn't want any more of Dad's insults.

Of course, Dad had cleaned up the kitchen by now. He and Melody were upstairs in her room, reading a book. I heard Melody giggle a few times. *If I were good in school, he would like me too,* I thought.

I went to bed with my Walkman on and listened to *Jane Eyre* as if it were a bedtime story. But when I turned the tape over, I heard some yelling. It was Dad, of course—shouting at Mom.

"What's going to happen when she has to line up with a bunch of other kids for a job, eh? What's she going to do then?" Guess who Dad was talking about—me.

Mom was keeping her voice down, so I couldn't hear her answer.

"That's out of the question!" Dad was on a roll now. "She has to take courses that lead to a high school diploma, and she's failing English. There's no room for some dumb auto course."

"She wants to be a mechanic!" Mom raised her voice, too.

"I don't care what she wants. She's

just lazy. There's probably no homework in auto shop."

So much for my sixteenth birthday present.

Sixteen—would that be old enough to get married? Hank had said to wait another year and then he would ask Dad, but why should we wait? In two weeks I'd be sixteen, and then maybe Hank wouldn't have to ask.

What would it be like to be married? Would things be different if I could quit school? At least nobody would care if I couldn't read.

For some reason that picture of Sleeping Beauty came to my mind. Maybe Hank was the prince I was waiting for.

And then, while thinking all those mixed-up thoughts, I fell asleep.

CHAPTER
5

The next day, I was going to listen to *Jane Eyre* as I walked to school.

"Shari, take those earphones off, please. It isn't safe—you won't hear cars or anything," Mom told me.

"O.K.," I said. I just wanted to hear the next chapter. My oral report was due in a week and I thought I could come up with a speech. But my biggest problem was the test Mr. Fulmer was going to give. What could I do about that?

I tried really hard to listen in class. I raised my hand and answered questions whenever I could. Teachers always liked that. When I handed in my rotten test answers, I'd need Mr. Fulmer to like me.

The other kids at school all used *Coles Notes,* but those wouldn't help me much. I tried to ask around, see what the others in my class thought would be on the test. That's when I found out how Drew could afford the gas for his Trans Am.

"Hey, Fix-it Lady," he called to me, grinning. "Heard you're in a sweat about Old Man Fulmer's test."

I nodded.

"For thirty bucks," he said, "I can help you get cool."

"How?" I asked.

"I'll get you a copy of the test," he answered, moving in closer.

So—Drew was the guy who supplied the school with sheets. In every school I'd been to there was someone like him.

"Thirty bucks! That's too much!" I cried, but what choice did I have? I could just see my dad's face when I brought home another failing mark in English. "O.K.," I said. "When can I have it?"

"Meet me at my locker tomorrow morning with the cash." He twisted a strand of my hair around his finger.

"See you tomorrow then," I said, and pulled away.

After school, I met Hank at the new Mexican restaurant near the garage. Since I was grounded, we had to see each other before Dad came home.

I love Mexican food so I was in a good mood when we walked into the place. My friend Lyn was there with a lot of other kids from school having tacos and Coke. She gave me a thumbs-up sign when she saw me with Hank. The other girls were looking at Hank too, and I was proud to be with him.

We sat down and I pretended to look at the menu. The waitress came right over and Hank told her he'd have the Number Three.

I followed down the menu with my finger. GROUND FEED OR CHICKEN SPIRITS was all I could make out of his choice.

"Will that be the ground beef or the chicken strips on the burrito?" the waitress asked.

"Ground beef, please," Hank told her.

"And do you want the hot sauce and refried beans with that?" she went on.

"Yes, thank you," Hank answered.

"I'll have the same—except with the chicken strips." I might have liked something else, but I didn't have all day to figure out what else was on the menu. Then I asked the waitress where the washroom was.

"To your left at the end of that hall over there," she said, pointing the way.

I walked to where she pointed. *Left, left,* I wondered to myself and quickly checked which wrist my watch was on. I kept it on my left wrist.

Now the hard part—at the end of the

hall there were three doors. None of them had the usual picture of a girl or guy. None of them had the word "Ladies" either.

I waited awhile to see if I could follow someone in. Finally a woman walked toward one and I followed her through.

"Hey, can't you read—the sign says private," she said. She jabbed a finger in the air toward the little sign above my head.

No! No! I can't read! I wanted to scream, but of course I couldn't. "Sorry, I didn't see it," I mumbled and ducked out.

Now there were two doors left, and both had words that looked almost the same. I stared back and forth at the two words till the letters swam. One word was longer. Maybe in Spanish the word for Gentlemen was longer than Ladies, like in English. I pushed through the door with the short word, but I was wrong again. A guy turned to face me. It was Drew.

"Hey, Fix-it Lady, you're in the Señor's room. The Señora's room is next door—if *that's* what you're looking for."

I dashed out quickly, hearing laughter even after I made it to the ladies' room. I

stayed in there a long time to avoid seeing Drew, but it didn't help. He was waiting for me in the hall when I came out.

"Listen, Fix-it Lady. I could use some cash, like right away. Do you have the money now?"

"Not on me. I'll have to ask my friend," I said.

"O.K., I'm over in the booth by the window." He walked toward it as I went back to Hank.

"Shari, what took you so long? The food's here." He waited till I sat down before he added, "I saw you talking to that guy, Drew."

I bit into what would have been a great burrito.

"You wouldn't have anything to do with him if you knew the kind of guy he is. Can you believe he once offered me a copy of a math test to pay for an oil change?"

The burrito didn't taste so great all of a sudden. Over Hank's shoulder, I saw Drew looking to see if I was coming. I shook my head to signal that I couldn't. There was no way I could ask Hank for the money now.

CHAPTER

Next morning I rushed to Drew's locker with the money. Drew was reading out loud from a copy of *Playboy* magazine. "Patti Living. Bust 37, waist 24 and hips 34, likes to watch men play sports." I stood by like a jerk while he opened the centrefold.

"Whooooeeee," he said to the friends gathered around him.

"Drew, can I see you—alone," I broke in. I knew he was doing all this just to bug me.

"Excuse me, guys, the Fix-it Lady wants to see me—*alone.*"

His friends left, giggling and elbowing each other.

"I needed the money *last* night," Drew said as I dug into my purse.

"I'm sorry. My friend couldn't lend it to me, but I've got it now," I told him.

"I've got a better idea," he said as a slow grin crept across his face. "How about coming out with me tonight?"

What would I have to pay then?

"Drew, I'm going out with someone."

"Your 'friend', eh? Hank Vandyke. No wonder you couldn't get the money," Drew said, shaking his head. "Fine," he tossed a key at me. "Top left-hand drawer of Old Man Fulmer's desk. If you ask real nice maybe Vandyke can get the test for you."

Drew knew I couldn't ask Hank, but could I steal the test myself? No. No, of course not. I slipped the key in my jeans pocket and wondered what to do next.

When I got home that night, there was a strange noise coming from the top of the stairs.

"Melody?" I called out.

"There's something wrong with the

vac," Melody yelled down to me.

"Turn it off," I shouted, "before you burn out the motor."

"Can you fix it?"

"I won't know until I look at it," I answered.

With a screwdriver, it was easy enough to take the small machine apart. Some pieces of red yarn were wound around the roller and I cut them all off.

"Rug-hooking yarn?"

Melody blushed.

The black belt linking the roller to the

motor had snapped. "I'll have to put in a new belt, but I'll get it to work again."

"Thanks. You won't tell Dad, will you?"

"Not if you do me a little favour, and type something for me."

Melody made a face, but she said yes. I got a spare belt from the kitchen drawer.

Dad came home before I finished.

"Shari, what are you doing?" he said as he came up the stairs.

"Oh, well . . . fixing the vacuum cleaner." I don't know why I felt guilty about it.

"I can see that," he said, looking at the small pile of yarn on the floor. He took the screwdriver out of my hand and screwed the cover back on for me. "Mom tells me you want to take a course in auto mechanics next term."

I nodded.

"Look, I figure you want to take the course because it doesn't have a lot of homework. Or maybe because of Hank. But what do I know?" he said, shrugging his shoulders. "Prove me wrong. You can take that course if you bring your English mark up to 70 per cent. O.K.?"

If only I could. "I'll try, Dad," I said.

"That's my girl!" he said, putting his arm around my shoulders. I couldn't remember the last time he did that.

How could I ever get 70 per cent? I wanted to take auto mechanics so much. I put my hand in my pocket and touched the key to Mr. Fulmer's desk. That's when I knew—I would have to steal the test myself.

That night Melody typed out my report on *Jane Eyre*. I told her what to type, but it was hard for her and she made lots of mistakes.

I looked over the paper, pretending I could read it.

"Use your dictionary to check your spelling," Mr. Fulmer had told us when he gave out the topic. That was O.K. when you knew which words you couldn't spell. All the words looked scrambled to me. "Looks great, Melody. Thanks a lot."

My next problem was to get hold of that English test. I was edgy for days waiting for the right moment. Then I got a lucky break. At the end of an English class, the intercom crackled on, "Mr. Fulmer, come to the office please. Mr. Fulmer."

Great! I stayed behind gathering my books till no one was left in the classroom. Then I walked up to his desk. Now which was the left-hand drawer? I checked my wrists for my watch. Quickly I slipped the key into the slot of the drawer on that side and turned.

Someone coughed behind me. My heart stopped.

"Doin' your own dirty work, eh?"

Drew said with a grin.

"Just leave me alone," I whispered at him. I opened the drawer and flipped through the files.

"That's the one," Drew said when I got to a page with letters circled in red pen. I tried to copy the letters on to my hand, but the b and d answers slowed me down. I always had to stop and think about which side the stick was on. When it was on my watch side it was a b, otherwise it was a d.

There were footsteps coming down the hall. Drew snatched out the key and I

quickly shut the drawer.

"What's going on here?"

This time it was Mr. Fulmer.

CHAPTER

7

"Careful, sir, don't step there!" Drew said as he dropped to his knees beside me. "Did you find it yet?" he asked me.

I couldn't say a word, but I didn't have to.

"Shari lost her contact lens, sir. She was rubbing her eye, so she thought it dropped somewhere near."

Mr. Fulmer's words still rang in my ears. *What's going on here?* Stealing, lying, and soon cheating—that's what was going on here. All because I couldn't read the way other kids could.

Mr. Fulmer began looking around the

floor with Drew.

"Never mind. It's O.K.," I said when my heart started beating again. All that and I'd only gotten four answers.

I felt so rotten then I had to cut my next class. As if that would make things better.

I walked around to the back of the school to scoot out the gate. Then I caught sight of a 1967 Ford Mustang that was parked in the auto shop. The shop door was open and the guys in the class were working on the body. I wanted to be working on it too. I'd heard they had put in a rebuilt engine, and replaced two doors and all the fenders.

If I could pull off a 70 per cent, next term *I* might be working on a car like that. I'd be good at it, too. I wouldn't have to lie or cheat. I would love auto mechanics and Hank could always help me with that kind of reading.

When the bell rang, I stopped in the office to get the late pass that would let me into my next class. The secretary looked at me over half-glasses.

"Umm, I had trouble with my contact

lens," I said as I looked down at my feet. "I mean, I lost one and then found it and then . . . ." The lies were coming a little easier.

"All right, here you go," she said, handing me the slip.

The rest of the day I played the game, straining to remember what the teachers were saying. I raised my hand for every question. At last school was out and I was on my way home.

"Hey, Fix-it Lady, wait up." It was Drew's voice.

I kept walking, but he ran to catch up with me.

"Hey, relax. I just want to give you a little present." He waved a paper in the air with some circles on it. It was a copy of the answer sheet.

I swallowed hard. I tried to calm down—not to show how much I wanted that paper.

"You still want these English answers?" Drew asked with a grin. "What are you willing to give me for them?"

I fumbled quickly in my purse for money. "Thirty dollars, that's what you

said, wasn't it?" I held out the money, my
hand shaking.

Drew put his hand over mine for a
minute and then took the money. I
snatched the paper out of his other hand.

"Don't be in such a hurry," he winked.

"I have to go see Hank now. Thanks,
Drew," I said, backing away.

I walked quickly then—putting school
and Drew far behind me.

Hank was still working when I got to
Vandyke's Garage. He wiped his hands
with the rag hanging out of his pocket
and he took my hand. He had a sure and

firm grip that seemed to steady me. But I was so confused—should I marry him?

"Hank, do you love me?" I looked straight into his blue eyes.

"Yes," he answered quickly—so sure of himself.

"No matter what?"

"Hmm. Well, yes, but I know what kind of person you are. You love God and you're decent and all that's part of what I love."

I didn't really know how I felt about God sometimes, and I didn't feel decent with a cheat sheet in my purse. Yet

Hank was certain, so certain. "And you really would marry me?" I asked.

"I'd marry you today if you were old enough," he said. "Why all the questions?"

"It's just that I can't do well in school and it makes me feel rotten."

"You're so beautiful." He kissed me then and I felt wonderful again. Would I feel this great all the time if I were married to Hank?

I didn't know, until right then, how much the idea was growing on me. Getting married—it seemed so much easier than getting 70 per cent.

CHAPTER
8

Then it came time to give my report on *Jane Eyre*. Of course I couldn't read my report like the others did, so I had to know what I was going to say. I learned my report by heart, listening to Melody read it a few times. Then I practised the report back on her. It cost me five bucks, but it was worth it.

Finally I gave the report in front of the class. I looked down and moved my eyes to make like I was reading. What a relief to get it over with. Mr. Fulmer asked me a few questions, but I didn't mind—I felt as if I had read the book. I loved that story because I was like Jane Eyre—alone, confused.

I answered his questions and Mr. Fulmer look pleased. "Well done, Shari. You really understood the story," Mr. Fulmer said as he held out his hand for the written report. He gave it a quick glance, but made no comment.

Mr. Fulmer didn't like some of the book reports. Drew read his and it sounded like he had copied the report from somewhere. Had he even thought about what he'd written? When Mr. Fulmer asked him questions, he just bluffed his way through.

Still, I envied Drew. Dumb and greasy as he was, he could *read*. When he wrote the English test the next day, he would at least pass.

Not me.

Even though I knew which letters to circle, I had to take my time. I had to work slowly and not give answers for the wrong questions. And there were the b's and d's with their sticks jumping from one side to the other.

I wrote so that all the letters looked a lot alike. My spelling mistakes wouldn't show that way, but my hands got sweaty and my writing got smudgy. My test paper was a mess—like all my tests. Still, there was a chance I could get that 70 per cent.

A week later Mr. Fulmer called me aside and asked me, "Shari, did you ever find your contact lens?"

"No, and it's the third one I've lost. I just can't tell my dad." One more lie.

"Well Shari, if that's your problem, perhaps you should wear glasses." Then he gave me back my test. Even with

cheating I'd only got 52. "I couldn't make much sense of the written answers on your test," Mr. Fulmer said. Then he stopped and just looked at me. "Shari, if there's some other problem . . . maybe I could help."

He means it, I thought, *but what can he do?* "I'll do better next time," I said. That's what teachers liked to hear. It's what I always said, but I wasn't sure that Mr. Fulmer believed me.

Then later that day something awful happened—Drew got called to the office. All the kids were talking about it.

"Psst, did you hear? They found out about his cheat sheets."

"Yeah, I wonder if he's selling out all his customers now."

I felt sick listening to the rumours, but at supper time I felt even sicker. Ms. Nor, the principal, had called Dad at his office.

"Shari, can you tell me what she wants to see me about?" Dad asked me. "She didn't want to discuss it over the phone."

My heart pounded and my face burned. What could I tell him?

"I . . . I'm not sure." Chicken.

"Fine. Don't tell me." Dad closed his

eyes and leaned his head on his hand, then rubbed his forehead with his fingers. "I'll find out soon enough," he sighed. He stood up and walked to the garbage. Scrape, scrape—in went most of his supper.

When Mom walked through the door, she couldn't even set her briefcase down.

"There's no time to eat," Dad told her, "we have to meet with Shari's principal in ten minutes."

Mom closed her mouth and stared at me. They took off in a hurry and I was left alone with my sister.

Run, I thought.

"How come you're in trouble?" Melody asked.

"I cheated."

Melody gasped, "But why, Shari?"

I felt I had to explain to her. "I cheated, Melody, because I can't read."

She just stared at me, her mouth open as if she couldn't believe what I said.

"Now I have to get out of here," I told her as I tore away from her. "And fast too—before they get back."

"You can't go, Shari," she begged.

"I *have* to—I just can't face Dad," I

said, hugging her. "Can't you see?"

But she couldn't.

I took a breath, then spoke softly, "C'mon Melody, let's find you something good on TV."

She settled down on the couch and stared at the set. I left her watching rock videos, but with tears in her eyes.

I went back to my room and put Fluffy into my bed. If my parents just glanced in the room, they might think I was asleep. That would buy some more time.

Time to do what?

CHAPTER

I ran straight to the Vandyke's Garage, and got there just as Hank was locking up. He saw the look on my face. "Shari, what's wrong?"

"Could we drive somewhere—to talk?" I said.

"O.K., sure," he said, a little confused.

I got into the front of The Heap. He started the engine and we drove around while I tried to find the words to tell him.

"Let's go somewhere quiet, Hank."

There were a hundred questions in Hank's eyes, but he knew not to ask them just then.

After a while we parked near the river. Now Hank turned to face me, thinking maybe I would explain.

I looked into his blue eyes. If only I could have kept that moment. Hank loved me. And I loved him—didn't I?

I lay my head against his chest and spoke softly, "Hank, listen to me."

Hank said nothing, but I knew he was listening to every word.

"I want to get married," I whispered.

"Me too, Shari," Hank answered—but he meant *some* day.

"I mean right away. But I guess there's . . . there's something I have to tell you." I couldn't go on, but I knew I couldn't stop either.

I held my breath. "Hank, I . . . I can't read."

Hank pulled me more tightly to his chest.

"That's why I have so much trouble in school. And I've been trying my best . . . but it's impossible.

"That doesn't matter to me," Hank said.

But I had to tell him the rest—before someone else did. "I bought test answers off of Drew, and now, somehow—I've been caught. Probably I'll be kicked out . . . Ms. Nor's talking to my parents right now."

"You cheated?" Hank stiffened and moved away from me. "And now you want to run away—you want me to marry you so you won't have to face your father." He made it sound awful.

"No, Hank, I . . . love you. I thought you loved me too."

"Are you sure—or are you lying to make things easier for yourself?"

"I never made it easier for myself!" I cried. "Don't you think it would have been easier to let them all know?"

"C'mon Shari—cheating? What kind of person are you?" His voice was cold—so cold that I just couldn't take it any more.

I got out of the car and slammed the door. Hank didn't try to stop me.

I felt rotten, but in a funny way I felt better than before. I wasn't lying any more. *I can't read!* I wanted to shout at the moon. It wasn't a guilty secret now.

I walked on, quickly—but where was I going? Back home? Yes, I realized—now it was time to face Mom and Dad. I had to tell them.

Hank pulled up beside me in The Heap. "C'mon, Shari, I can't let you walk home alone."

"Go away! I don't need you," I told him.

Hank moved The Heap forward as I kept walking. He pushed the door open, shouting, "Shari, will you just get back in!"

I hated the tone of his voice. I stopped, put my hands on my hips, and looked straight into his eyes. "No!" I said, and then turned away.

About half an hour passed. I was walking around a bend in the road when Dad's New Yorker tore up the street. It screeched to a stop across from me, and the window rolled down.

"Get in," he said.

I did as he told me, and we shot off toward home.

"What do you mean by running away?" Dad sputtered.

"Dad, I can't read," I said softly.

Dad ignored me and kept talking, "And that principal, do you know what she said? That you cheated on an exam. And instead of punishing you, she wants you to take some tests."

"I can't read," I said louder, so he had to hear me.

"Your English teacher thinks you have 'learning problems', but that's crazy. No one in our family ever had 'learning problems.' "

"Dad, are you listening?" I yelled at him. "I can't read!"

We were in the driveway. Dad shut the engine off and wrenched the handbrake on. He said nothing for a few moments, then he looked over at me. "It can't be true."

I ran into the house crying.

Mom caught me in her arms. "Mom, it's not my fault—I can't read," I sobbed.

"What are they teaching in schools anyway?" Dad muttered as he stormed past us and up into their bedroom.

"It's O.K., Shari," Mom said, hugging me so tightly I could hardly breathe. Then she let go. "This isn't the kind of thing you can hide or run away from."

"I know that now, Mom. . . . But what's going to happen to me?"

CHAPTER

10

The first thing that happened was that I had to meet with Ms. Nor and Mr. Fulmer. Then I went through two days of tests. I hate tests and they were awful.

A few days later Mr. Fulmer explained the results to me. "Shari, have you ever heard of dyslexia?"

I shook my head.

"It means . . . when you're trying to read, your eyes see the letters all right. But when the picture gets to your brain . . . well, the wires are crossed and somehow the picture gets scrambled. We really don't know why this happens to some people—"

He stopped like he expected me to say something. I just stared.

"But for now, you can tape your lessons. Your teachers will let you do your exams out loud until you can read better. And Shari . . . ," he stopped for a moment and smiled, ". . . you *will* read better. You'll have a special teacher who will spend time with you every day. I know you can work around those crossed wires."

The special teacher thought so too. She told me that looking at my watch to tell my left hand from my right hand was called a "coping skill." She said she would teach me more coping skills that would help me read.

That lunch hour Lyn came up to me with another Sun Valley High paperback.

"Lyn, I'm dyslexic—I mean, I can't read. There's no point in me taking these books."

"You mean you've never read any of them?" she asked.

"I couldn't. Anyhow, I'll give you back your books," I said.

"Why don't you keep them until you *can* read?"

I smiled. That really wasn't so bad.

Then my birthday came around. We had a party with pizza for supper and the usual birthday cake and candles.

When we were done eating, Melody put a blindfold on me and led me to my present. We stopped in Mom's office and the blindfold came off.

TO SHARI, HAPPY SIXTEENTH BIRTHDAY. The words were in light green letters on a screen. It took me a while to figure it out. "My own computer?" I asked.

"Yeah, and you should see the great games we can play on it," Melody said.

"There's a spelling checker that comes with it," Dad said. "It's to help you with your, uh, problem." Dad blushed and I got the feeling he was trying to tell me something more. He pressed a few keys and a picture of a car formed on the screen. Then a wrench beside it. "Your birthday card," he said, smiling.

"That's decent!" Melody cried out.

I thought it was more than decent,

since I guessed what the picture on the screen meant.

"I don't see why you can't take that auto mechanic's class you wanted, Shari," Dad said.

"Now can I give her my present?" Melody broke in. Dad nodded and she gave me a small package. "It was Dad's idea, but I paid for it," she said proudly.

"Big surprise," Mom said. "She wouldn't even tell *m e* what she got you."

Jewellery? I opened the package and found a set of keys.

"They're keys to the New Yorker," Melody said with a grin.

I gaped and stared—first at the keys, then at Dad.

"Most people know how to drive cars before they learn how to fix them. A friend of mine owns a driving school and you're signed up."

My mouth still hung open.

"I don't believe it," Mom said to Melody and me. "He doesn't even like *m e* to drive his car. You never told me," she said to Dad, and then she threw me another small package. "Oh well, great minds think alike."

Jewellery was not the kind of present
my mother would give me. I tore off the
wrapping paper to—another set of car
keys! This time for the Subaru.

We all laughed and I felt great. But
then the doorbell rang and I went to
answer it.

It was Hank. That scene in the car had
been a week ago, and I hadn't spoken to
him since. He didn't look the same to me
any more. Maybe it was because he was
all dressed up, or maybe it was because
of what happened between us.

He handed me sixteen roses.

"Thanks, I'll put them in water," I said as he shifted from one foot to the other. "Mom, Dad, it's Hank," I called out.

"Go ahead and take a drive. It's your birthday," Dad groaned. He was starting to sound more like himself.

"Thanks, Dad. We won't be long."

We drove to the river and parked. When Hank leaned over to kiss me, I wanted to move away.

I guess Hank must have sensed how I felt. He put a small wrapped package in my hand, but I knew his present wouldn't be a set of keys to The Heap. Slowly I peeled up the edges of the tape and undid the wrapping paper. Inside was a little blue box. When I lifted the lid, I found a ring—not a diamond—but a small pearl set on a silver band.

"We can't get married without your parents' O.K. till you're nineteen. I checked," Hank said.

I didn't take the ring from the box.

"Your dad wouldn't let me buy you a diamond for at least one more year. He also said women like to pick their own engagement rings." Hank stopped and

smiled. "Can we call this our pre-engagement ring?"

I shook my head.

"Look, Shari," he said. "I've forgiven you for cheating at school . . . ."

"You've forgiven *me*, Hank?" I sputtered. All the anger from that night suddenly came back to me.

Hank looked stunned.

"I don't want to marry you any more," I said. The moment I said it out loud, I knew it was true.

"But Shari, I love you," Hank whispered.

"But do you really love *me,* Hank?"

"I don't care what you did, Shari—I love you."

I closed my eyes and remembered that night when I told him I had cheated. Then I had needed him to tell me those words, but now it just wasn't the same.

"But I don't love you, Hank," I said, finally getting out the toughest part. His eyes were filling. I stopped being mad at him and that made it even tougher. "So I can't take this ring." I pushed it back to him.

I wanted to hold him and make him feel better, the way he had for me so many times. But I couldn't pretend—no more lying, no more cheating.

We drove back to my house and parked. Hank kept begging me to take the ring, to think it over, but to keep the ring, no matter what. He tugged at my hand and whispered, "Please, Shari."

I just couldn't. I didn't want to cry, so I shook my head, got out of the car and closed the door.

CHAPTER

11

Dad took the morning off work to take me for my learner's permit. His friend at the driving school had coached me on the Driver's Handbook and had set up an oral test.

It took about a half an hour and I hated it—but I passed. Dad beamed and kissed me. "Great job, Shari. I just hope you don't mind if I drive until you've had a few lessons."

I shook my head. Mom and I still secretly thought he'd never let me drive the New Yorker.

We weren't too far from home when I

saw Drew's orange Trans Am parked, hood up, on the street outside his house.

What was wrong with his car now? I wanted to drive right by him. Stupid turkey! But then that word "stupid" made me think about how I'd felt about myself—until I found out that I was dyslexic.

Drew really did seem slow, and I hated his greasy comments. But what if there was something just a little different about his brain, too? I mean he could read, but maybe he couldn't remember things. Maybe he acted like a big sleaze to cover up his problem. No one could help the way their brain worked.

That made me change my mind and ask Dad to stop. "He's a friend from school. I'll just see if it's something simple," I said, getting out of the car.

"What's wrong, Drew?"

"Fix-it Lady! If I knew, I wouldn't be standing here, eh? I turn the key and there's just a click and then nothing."

As I walked around the Trans Am I saw the problem. Up front Drew was trying my pen trick with his choke.

"Hey, Drew, your last date must have

left in a real hurry." I pointed to a seat belt hanging out from the passenger door, which was slightly open. "I bet your dome light's been on all night and now your battery's dead. I'll get my dad's jumper cables out."

Drew's face went red. It felt great to embarrass him for a change.

I thought Dad would get out and connect up the cables, but no, he just moved the car in a little closer.

When I had the cables in place, I signalled for Dad to rev his engine. Then I nodded to Drew, who turned the key. The Trans Am roared to life.

"Uh, hmm, thanks, Shari," Drew said, using my real name for the first time ever.

"That's O.K.," I said as I took off the cables.

"I . . . I'm sorry about ratting on you about the English test and all," Drew told me in a low voice, so Dad couldn't hear. "I thought they already knew about you or I wouldn't have." I could see he really was sorry. "Hey, hope I can give you a jump start some time too, Fix-it Lady."

I looked into his eyes for a clue. Was he

making one more sleazy remark? I couldn't tell. But if it weren't for him, who knows if Mr. Fulmer would have told Ms. Nor about my problem. I might still be struggling to get by in school. Was Drew the prince who had rescued me? Nah, not Drew, and not Hank either. Princes only solve problems in fairy tales.

I smiled back at him. "You've already given me a jump start, Drew, even if you don't know it."

He shrugged his shoulders and drove off.

I got back into the car with Dad.

"You never could pass by an open hood, could you?" Dad turned to me. "You know—deep down I think I always knew you had some kind of problem in school. Oh, Shari, I'm sorry." Dad's voice cracked. "I just couldn't admit it—not my own perfect girl. You were never lazy at home—why would I think you were lazy at school?"

Dad stopped to clear his throat and wiped some wetness from under his eyes. Then he went on, "I still hate the thought of you being a mechanic. An

engineer, I could see that, but . . . ." Dad sounded like his old self again. He broke off and blushed. "But if you want to be a mechanic, if you *really* want to be a mechanic—you'll be the one to get all my business."

I couldn't say anything back to him. Not without crying. And crying is a dumb thing to do when you're happy.

About the Author

Sylvia McNicoll lives in Burlington, dividing her time between chauffeuring and custodial duties for her husband and three children—and writing.

A former student of Paul Kropp's, she has written two other novels so far: *The Tiger Catcher's Kid* and *Blueberries and Whipped Cream*.

Acknowledgements

For all of you, especially Jason, Jeremy, and Jody.

A special thanks to Aleya and her mom, Sarah Bunnett-Gibson, Learning Disabilities Association of Ontario, for their input. Also Glenn Woods for using Editorial Psychology 101 when it was necessary.

If you enjoyed this book,
you may also enjoy reading . . .

BABY, BABY
When two people love each other, anything they do is
all right. That's what Dave tells Lori. But when Lori
gets pregnant, they find out that love is not enough.

FIRE! FIRE!
Deea joined the crew to fight forest fires. She didn't
expect to have to fight her boss, too. She knew it was
dangerous to follow Good Boy's orders. And now she
is trapped in a blazing fire—with him.

HEAD LOCK
Peter Mills feels like a loser until he signs up with
the wrestling team. Then Peter surprises
everyone—his parents, his friends, even himself—
as he fights his way to the finals.

ICE HAWK
Ice Hawk's break into big time hockey is a dream
come true. But the coach wants a goon—not a stick
star—and the dream turns into a nightmare.

NINE LIVES
Cat has always been curious, and her summer job at
the resort makes it easy to snoop. But this time Cat's
snooping gets her in real trouble—and might cost
her even more than nine lives.

TOUGH STUFF
Nikki was always tough—even after the judge made
her do volunteer work at the hospital. Nikki wasn't
going to let that change her. She'd show Jake and
the gang just how tough she really was.

WILD NIGHT
The night shift at the 7 Eleven may not be the greatest job—but it pays. Mostly, there isn't much for Tony to do. Until one night when . . . it all goes wild.

WILD ONE
Kate saves Wild One from Banner's whip and gets to train the horse herself. But that's only a start. Can she prove he can race before it's too late?

Have you heard of **Series 2000?**

Death Wind by William Bell
In the Time of the Monsters by Martyn Godfrey
The Last War by Martyn Godfrey
More Than Weird by Martyn Godfrey
Bull Rider by Marilyn Halvorson
The Wimp and Easy Money by John Ibbitson
The Wimp and the Jock by John Ibbitson
Baby Blues by Paul Kropp
Death Ride by Paul Kropp
Jo's Search by Paul Kropp
Not Only Me by Paul Kropp
Under Cover by Paul Kropp

Note: Teacher's Guides for both **Series Canada** and **Series 2000** are also available.

For more information, write:
Collier Macmillan Canada, Inc.
1200 Eglinton Ave. East, Suite 200
Don Mills, Ontario M3C 3N1
or call: **(416) 449-6030**